Linda Shelmandine is a retired English teacher living in Newburgh, NY. She has written *The Goode Sisters* not only as a supporter of the LGBT community but also as one who has a heart for children and shares the hope we all have in them for a better tomorrow.

The Goode Sisters

A Children's Tale for Parent and Child about Gender Identity

Linda Shelmandine

AUSTIN MACAULEY PUBLISHERS™

LONDON · CAMBRIDGE · NEW YORK · SHARJAH

Copyright © Linda Shelmandine (2020)

The right of **Linda Shelmandine** to be identified as author of this work has been asserted by the author in accordance with section 77 and 78 of the Copyright, Designs and Patents Act 1988.

All rights reserved. No part of this publication may be reproduced, stored in a retrieval system, or transmitted in any form or by any means, electronic, mechanical, photocopying, recording, or otherwise, without the prior permission of the publishers.

Any person who commits any unauthorised act in relation to this publication may be liable to criminal prosecution and civil claims for damages.

A CIP catalogue record for this title is available from the British Library.

ISBN 9781528973335 (Paperback)
ISBN 9781528973359 (ePub e-book)

www.austinmacauley.com

First Published (2020)
Austin Macauley Publishers Ltd
25 Canada Square
Canary Wharf
London
E14 5LQ

To Vanessa, who started me down this road.

I wish to thank James, who — always wanting best for me — has supported and assisted me ever so patiently with the submission process and throughout the particulars of the publishing process. I also wish to thank all those at Austin Macauley who made this publication possible.

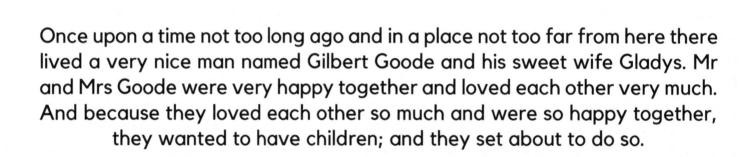

Once upon a time not too long ago and in a place not too far from here there lived a very nice man named Gilbert Goode and his sweet wife Gladys. Mr and Mrs Goode were very happy together and loved each other very much. And because they loved each other so much and were so happy together, they wanted to have children; and they set about to do so.

As the months passed, Mr and Mrs Goode would often sit on their porch in the cool evening and talk about the children they would have and what a happy family they would be.

And although Mrs Goode was not so sure, Mr Goode was absolutely, positively, *definitely* sure that their first child was going to be a *boy*! And because Mr Goode was so absolutely, positively, *definitely* sure, he already had a name picked out, Gaither. Yes, Gaither.

A few more months passed, and in the summer when the honey bees were buzzing and the air was warm and heavy, Gladys Goode gave birth...to...a... *girl*! "Well, what d'ya know", smiled Mr Goode. However, as her parents thought about it, it seemed to them a perfectly good name after all. And, as they had thought of their first child as Gaither for so long, the daughter was given the name anyway! So, Gaither she was, and Gaither she stayed.

However, Gaither, herself, chose at an early age to prove to everybody and everyone that, although she was given a name in her own mind that was more suited for a boy, she *indeed* was a girl! So, she clothed herself in all things she considered *girly* — flowers and ribbons and curls and anything pink all the time, everywhere, regardless of the weather, the day of the week or the month of the year.

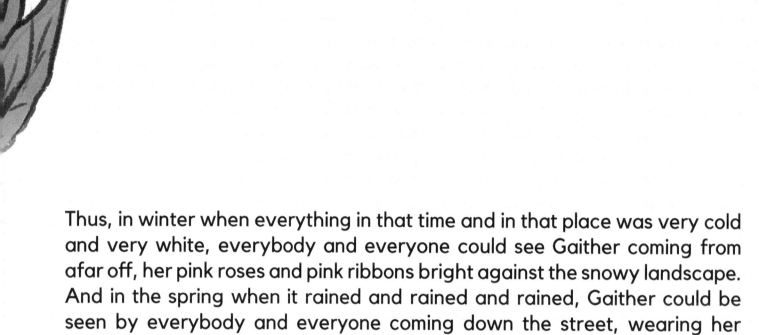

Thus, in winter when everything in that time and in that place was very cold and very white, everybody and everyone could see Gaither coming from afar off, her pink roses and pink ribbons bright against the snowy landscape. And in the spring when it rained and rained and rained, Gaither could be seen by everybody and everyone coming down the street, wearing her bright pink and pink striped rubber boots with her pink roses and her pink ribbons safe and dry beneath her huge rosy pink umbrella.

The really astonishing thing, though, was that although Gaither made a point to declare her femininity to everybody and everyone by what she wore, she seemed to have been born with an uncanny ability to figure out, and thus repair, 'All Things Mechanical', an ability that was quite unusual for a girl who lived in that time and in that place. Against this natural inclination Gaither did not struggle but embraced it gladly for she loved 'All Things Mechanical'.

So, after growing up building and fixing 'All Things Mechanical' for her family, it was only natural that Gaither would go into business fixing lawn mowers and chain saws and washing machines and automobiles for everybody and everyone. And when she set up shop in the old garage in the side yard, Gaither's 'Open for Business' sign hung over the pink garage doors and was itself painted a lovely pink with a rose in each corner.

By the time Gaither's baby sister came along, Mrs Goode was quite set on the name Linda for her second daughter. However, Mr Goode had settled in his own mind that all of his children would have a name that began with the letter 'G' so that their given names would sound most harmoniously with the name of 'Goode'. Mr and Mrs Goode, both possessing a compromising and happy temperament, happily compromised. So, Glinda the second daughter was, and Glinda she stayed.

14

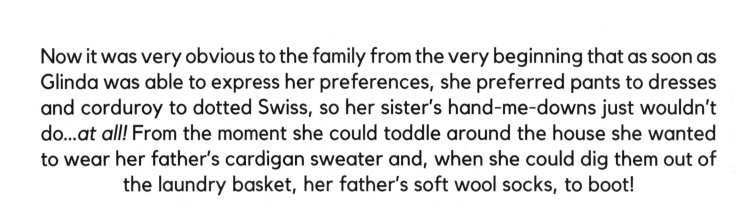

Now it was very obvious to the family from the very beginning that as soon as Glinda was able to express her preferences, she preferred pants to dresses and corduroy to dotted Swiss, so her sister's hand-me-downs just wouldn't do...*at all!* From the moment she could toddle around the house she wanted to wear her father's cardigan sweater and, when she could dig them out of the laundry basket, her father's soft wool socks, to boot!

Finally, because her parents were reasonable people and loved Glinda and wanted her to be happy, they went out and bought her the corded corduroy overalls she wanted and let her pick out some blue flannel shirts to wear under them and some soft cardigan sweaters to wear over them. And on her feet in all kinds of weather Glinda wore mud boots. Just mud boots with soft wool socks inside them. Although Glinda's clothes were considered by many in that time and in that place as unusual for a girl, many more others saw past Glinda's clothes to the happy and generous heart that beat beneath her flannel shirts and loved her for it.

Now Glinda was always hanging around her mother in the kitchen, peering from behind her mother's elbow as Mrs Goode rolled out the dough for breakfast biscuits or pulling a chair up to the table so she could see more clearly while her mother trimmed a pie crust. Glinda was intrigued by the magic of baking. Her mother would begin with two cups of this and one cup of that and after mixing and scraping and rolling out or pouring in, Mrs Goode would take it out of the oven, and voila! there would be 'Something Wonderful!'

Glinda watched and watched, and, finally, one day Mrs Goode asked her daughter if she would like to try baking 'Something Wonderful' herself. And from the moment Glinda picked up her first mixing spoon and poured her first two cups of flour into the bright red mixing bowl, she was in love with baking! And the cakes and cookies that Glinda made were so good that her mother would serve them to her friends when they came to visit, and the word soon got around to everybody and everyone that Glinda baked 'Something Wonderful' cookies and 'Something Wonderful' cakes, and voila! Glinda was now in business for herself just like her sister Gaither.

When it came time for the Goode's third child to be born it was spring, and the crape myrtle and the magnolia were lovely in bloom. And when another little girl was born Mr Goode thought it would be nice to name their lovely little girl after a flower. When Mrs Goode happily agreed, and because her given name must begin with a 'G' so it would sound harmoniously with the family name of Goode, it took a while to settle on a flower name for their new baby girl. Gerbere? Gladiolus? Godetia? "Good grief!" sighed Mrs Goode. Gardenia?

Gardenia! "How lovely!" sighed Mrs Goode. So, Gardenia she was, and Gardenia she stayed.

From the moment Gardenia could talk she showed her interest in flowers for her very first word was 'fow-wer'! She loved the shapes of flowers and the colours of flowers and the lovely smell of flowers. All these things made Gardenia VERY happy, and she very MUCH wanted to have her own garden. And when Gardenia was just a wee little girl, she did! Mr Goode made a small place on the corner of their lawn so Gardenia could plant her flowers.

In the beginning Mr and Mrs Goode had to help Gardenia pick out the proper seeds in The Garden Shop and to show her how to dig the right size hole in which to plant them. They taught her how much sun the flowers would need and how much water to give them.

But sooner than her parents expected Gardenia was making the choices all on her own and giving them the proper care until any garden that Gardenia planted and cared for was one of the prettiest everybody and everyone had ever seen!

And on the days when the sun was bright in the sky and the air was soft all around and Gardenia was feeling one with her garden, she could be seen trimming and weeding her garden, wearing one of Gaither's straw hats festooned with bright silk roses and pink ribbons that tied under her chin. And as the sun caught the lovely pink colours of her sister's dress, Gardenia would seem to disappear into the flower beds she was tending. And on the days when she was expanding her garden with digging and hauling and planting, Gardenia would wear a pair of Glinda's nice utilitarian overalls.

So, as the years passed, Gaither would happily repair 'All Things Mechanical' for everybody and everyone in her pink garage shop. Glinda would bake everybody and everyone 'Something Wonderful' tarts and pies and breads and cookies, and Gardenia would work and dance in her ever-expanding garden.

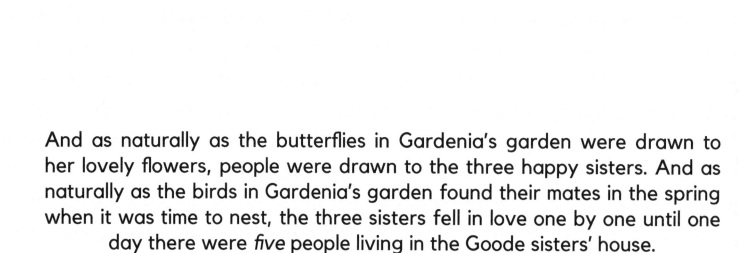

And as naturally as the butterflies in Gardenia's garden were drawn to her lovely flowers, people were drawn to the three happy sisters. And as naturally as the birds in Gardenia's garden found their mates in the spring when it was time to nest, the three sisters fell in love one by one until one day there were *five* people living in the Goode sisters' house.

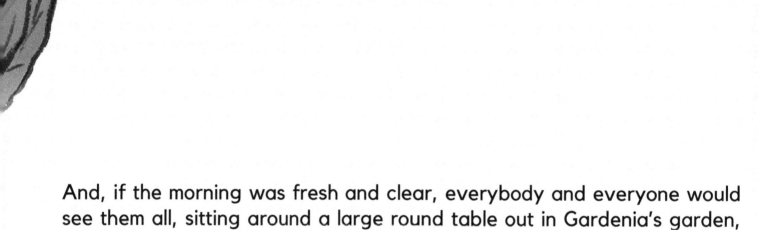

And, if the morning was fresh and clear, everybody and everyone would see them all, sitting around a large round table out in Gardenia's garden, having breakfast al fresco.

And Gaither and Glinda who each loved someone very special and very beautiful and were greatly loved in return were very, very happy. And when Gardenia fell in love with the large empty lot next door, and Gaither and Glinda bought it for her with some of the money they had earned from repairing and baking, Gardenia, herself, was also very, very happy for she had her *own* true love — her garden, her very special, very beautiful garden. There they all sat. Gaither who still wore pink ribbons and flowers in her hair sat next to Franklin. Glinda as comfortable as always in corduroy and mud boots sat with Anna. And smiling at all of them, sat Gardenia who loved her family and was happy in her garden.

So, this is the story of three sisters, each becoming what was there in the seed in the beginning like the flowers in Gardenia's garden. All colours. All kinds. All shapes and sizes. The garden made room for them all. There they lived side by side, making the garden a thing of true beauty.

CPSIA information can be obtained
at www.ICGtesting.com
Printed in the USA
BVHW020120021220
594663BV00010B/101